The House of Lost and Found

Story by Martin Widmark
Illustrations by Emilia Dziubak

Floris
Books

Niles was old. His eyesight was dim and his bones creaked.
He lived alone in an old, dim, creaky house. His pot plants
had withered. He never bothered opening the windows.
The cat, Johan Sebastian, grew tired of gloominess, and of Niles,
and one day he disappeared.

   Just as well, thought Niles. That's one less thing to worry about.

In the evening, Niles walked from room to room in the house turning off the lights. His children had grown up years ago. They lived far away now, and had their own children.

His wife, Sara, had died, so she wasn't there either, except in Niles's thoughts. He heard her call from her studio, "Niles! Come and look at this."

He opened the studio door. All her paintings still hung there.
"Do you like this one?" she asked.

It was a picture of a beautiful summer meadow covered in big red poppies.

The meadow was where they'd first walked together and fallen in love.

Niles murmured a reply to Sara and turned off the studio lamp.

He closed the studio door.

In his study he thought about the times when he used to sit and read in the comfy armchair. He ran his fingers along the spines of his books. They felt soft. And they smelled good.

He sighed and turned off the study light.

The children's room still had a bed for Michael and a bed for Elsa.
Michael was the eldest but he'd always wanted to share with his
sister. He'd been afraid of the dark, though he would never admit it.
    Niles turned off the lamp by their beds. He heard Michael whisper,
half-awake, "Leave it on a bit longer?" Elsa was already asleep.
    Niles tiptoed out.

Upstairs, Niles changed into his pyjamas.
He lay down in bed.
   He said goodnight to Sara.
   He gazed up at the ceiling.
   He was tired, so tired.
   He had turned off all the lights in the house, except the
bedroom light. He put his hand on the switch by the bed.
   That's when the doorbell rang.
   What? Who could this be? He must have imagined it.
   He sank back on his pillow and put his hand on the
light switch once more.
   The doorbell rang again.
   Niles sat up heavily and pulled on his dressing gown.
   "Who can be ringing the doorbell at this late hour?"
he muttered, as he stomped down the stairs. "Ridiculous!"

"*What* do you think—" Niles began. Then he saw a young boy standing outside the door, holding a flowerpot.

Niles unlocked the door. A blackbird sang in the sweet evening air.

"Hello!" said the boy.

"Mmm," replied Niles.

"I'm your next-door neighbour," continued the boy.

"Good neighbours don't disturb each other," answered Niles, "especially not at night."

The boy smiled. "I'm going on holiday," he said.

"How nice for you," Niles grumped.

"And I thought you could take care of my flower," continued the boy. He held out the pot. There was no flower to be seen, only dirt. "It has to be watered every day," he said.

Niles stood in the doorway holding the flowerpot. "I'm sorry," he called after the boy. "I can't take care of anything. It won't—"

But the boy had gone.

Niles stood for a long time with the flowerpot in his hands. I don't want this thing, he thought. Walking into the kitchen, he dumped the flowerpot on the table, and went to bed.

He turned off the bedroom light.

Dark.

Quiet.

"Stupid, wretched thing!" he said out loud.

He turned the bedroom light on again and stomped down to the kitchen. He stopped stomping to fill a watering can and gently wet the dirt in the pot. Then he looked angrily at it before stomping back upstairs and turning off his bedroom light.

The next morning, Niles slept late. When he woke, the sun was shining on the dirty bedroom windows. For some reason, he felt lighter – less gloomy than he'd been for a long time.

Then he remembered the flowerpot on the kitchen table, and his cheerful mood disappeared. He got dressed.

In the kitchen, the flowerpot stood where he'd left it.

He made coffee and took out two dry biscuits. "You can just stay where you are," he said over his shoulder to the flowerpot. "I didn't ask you to come." He sat down and drank the coffee and ate the biscuits. "I should really throw you out," he told the pot. "But that might upset the boy."

Then Niles caught sight of something.

He leaned closer to the flowerpot. His eyes were so dim.

He rushed to find his magnifying glass in the study. Back in the kitchen, he peered through it. Yes! A tiny fragile leaf was peeping out from the dirt in the pot.

Niles realised he hadn't asked the boy what kind of flower might grow.

He poured himself another cup of coffee and sniffed the air in the kitchen. "We need to freshen this room," he announced.

Niles finished his coffee and walked around the house opening every window. Warm, fragrant air rushed inside.

In the bright light, Niles noticed the dirty smears and dust on the windows. He got soapy water and a cloth and set to work.

That evening, when Niles turned off the bedroom light, he was still wondering what sort of flower was growing in the pot in the kitchen.

The next day, sun shone into the house through the sparkling clear
windows. Niles saw how dusty the corners of the rooms had become.
First a cup of coffee, then out with the broom and the mop, he thought.

But in the kitchen, he suddenly stopped in surprise.

There beside the flowerpot sat someone he knew.

"Johan Sebastian!" shouted Niles.

"Meow," replied the cat.

Niles stroked his purring cat and poured some cream into a saucer under the table. He and Johan Sebastian had breakfast together.

Niles saw that the little green shoot had pushed higher out of the dirt. He wondered again what kind of flower it would be. A violet? A geranium? A tulip?

After breakfast, Niles cleaned. He swept, washed and dusted.
He threw out dead plants and dried-up flowers. Johan Sebastian
watched curiously.

At last, after he'd even scrubbed the staircase, Niles stopped and
stretched. He wandered into the study and sank into his armchair.

His reading glasses were on the table. He gave them a polish and put them on. Then he took a book from the shelf.

That night, Johan Sebastian jumped onto the bed and curled himself into a ball by Niles's feet.
    Niles turned off the light, forgot to say goodnight to his wife, and fell deeply asleep.

The days passed. Niles cleaned, cooked and read, Johan Sebastian purred and the flower grew. Green leaves with frilly edges emerged from a long stalk, and a bud swelled rounder and rounder.

One afternoon, sitting at the kitchen table, Niles thought, I might redecorate the hallway. Perhaps with pale yellow wallpaper?

Then he caught sight of the round bud.

It had opened. A bright red petal peeped out.

"I knew it!" he said out loud. "You're a poppy!" It was just like the ones in the field Sara had painted, in the field where it all began.

Niles felt very happy. A tear ran down his cheek.

Then, the doorbell rang.

"We're home," said the boy.

Niles hurried to the kitchen to fetch the flowerpot.

"It's beautiful!" said the boy.

"It just opened," Niles told him. "It's a poppy."

The boy smiled. Niles handed him the flowerpot, and heaved a deep sigh.

The boy looked up. "My parents said to ask if you'd come and sit out in the garden with us?"

Niles could hear voices on the other side of the hedge. He thought for a moment. Then he said, "My name is Niles."

"Thanks for taking care of my flower, Niles," replied the boy. "Do you want to come?"

Niles nodded. "I'll get my jacket."

They set off together. Johan Sebastian padded along beside them, his tail held high in the warm golden air.